EnoRMoUS ELEPhanT

First published in 2008 by Hodder Children's Books
This paperback edition published in 2009

Text copyright © Bruce Hobson 2008
Illustrations copyright © Adrienne Kennaway 2008
www.brucehobson.net

Hodder Children's Books, 338 Euston Road, London, NW1 3BH

Hodder Children's Books Australia
Level 17/207 Kent Street, Sydney, NSW 2000

The right of Bruce Hobson to be identified as the author and
Adrienne Kennaway as the illustrator of this Work has been asserted
by them in accordance with the Copyright, Designs and Patents Act 1988.

A catalogue record of this book is available from the British Library.

ISBN: 978 0 340 94522 3

Printed in China

Hodder Children's Books is a division of Hachette Children's Books.
An Hachette UK Company.
www.hachette.co.uk

Enormous Elephant

Written by
Mwenye Hadithi

Illustrated by
Adrienne Kennaway

h
Hodder
Children's
Books

a division of Hachette Children's Books

In the days before the Big Rains many of the animals on the Great Plains looked very different.

Python was short and fat.

Ostrich had a short neck and very short legs.

And Elephant had a short stump of a nose and a short tuft for a tail, but a very **BIG** body.

"Elephant has such a short tail and such a small nose!" Python giggled. "And they're stuck on either end of such a large body!"

"It makes him look enormous!" laughed Ostrich.

"I'm not enormous," grumbled Elephant. "I'm just big. My nose is small and my tail is short so I look bigger than I am."

Since Elephant could only pick up a small amount of grass and water in his little trunk, he had to spend all day eating and drinking.

This made him look very greedy.

"I'm not greedy," grumbled Elephant. "There's just a lot of me to fill and I can only put in a small amount at a time."

So Enormous Elephant and his family spent
all their time going from lake to river to pond
and back again, drinking and eating for hours.
They travelled in a long line, each short tail
in front held by a small nose behind.

In Big Mud Lake there
lived a Very Large Crocodile.
Nobody had ever seen him, but
everybody knew he was there.

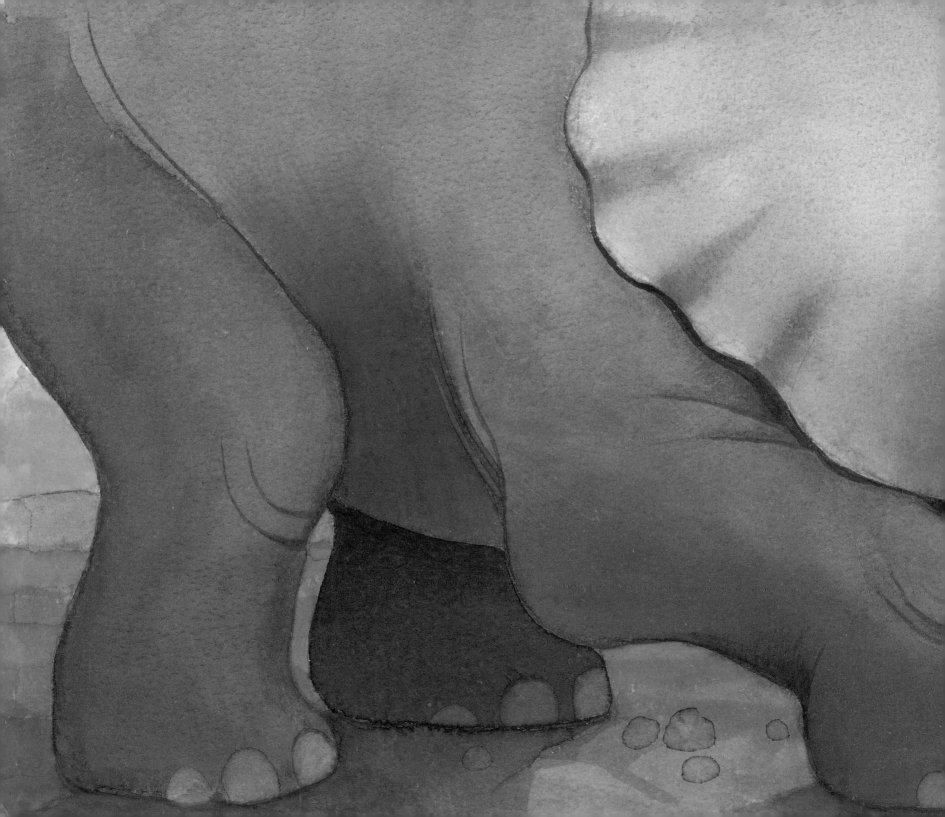

As the sun grew hotter, the rivers and ponds dried up. Soon the elephants could not find enough water to drink. So one evening, as they passed along the shores of Big Mud Lake, Enormous Elephant dipped his trunk in the water. Just the very tip. Just a little bit.

Now the water was so low that the bottom of the lake was rather close to the top, and Very Large Crocodile was only just covered by the shallow water.

Crocodile opened one eye and there he saw a small wriggling wiggler! So he opened his mouth and...

"HELfPf!" cried Enormous Elephant as he suddenly found his trunk was stuck. He tugged and he pulled, but it was trapped in the water.

Each elephant held fast
to the one in front.
Then the whole line of
elephants hauled and heaved,
but Enormous Elephant's
trunk was still stuck.

Ostrich was passing and took the tail of the last Elephant in her beak. She strained and she skidded, but Enormous Elephant's trunk would not budge.

"HELfPf!"

yelled Enormous Elephant.

Python was passing and held
tight to Ostrich's feet.
He tugged and he twisted,
but still Elephant's trunk
would not pull free.

Spider was passing and when she saw the animals in a long line, tugging and pulling, she spun a silver rope. She tied one end to Python's tail and the other end she wound round and round a Baobab tree.

Then, as the evening wind began to
blow strongly, the Baobab tree
leaned with the wind and the silver
rope began to tighten.

At the bottom of Big Mud Lake,
Very Large Crocodile felt his jaws
begin to ache. Since he was rather
attached to his teeth, he opened
them with a sudden

SNIKK!

And Enormous Elephant was free.

All the animals tumbled backwards in a heap.
They picked themselves up and dusted
themselves off, and then they began to laugh.
They had all been stretched and stretched!

Ostrich had a long thin neck. And such long legs she could run like the wind!

Python was long and smooth and snakelike. She could slide and stretch and slither!

And when they saw
Enormous Elephant with his
new long trunk and his fine
tail, they realised he wasn't
enormous after all.
He was just right.

On the Great Plains, Enormous
Elephant and his family showed off their
new trunks and tails to the other animals.

And every evening by Big Mud Lake, one more elephant would come and dip his trunk in the water. But just the very, very tip. Just a little tiny bit.

And to this day elephants tromp proudly across the Great Plains, waving their trunks and swishing their tails.